Ways to Go

BOATS GO!

By Sean MacDumont

Gareth Stevens
PUBLISHING

Please visit our website, www.garethstevens.com. For a free color catalog of all our high-quality books, call toll free 1-800-542-2595 or fax 1-877-542-2596.

Cataloging-in-Publication Data

Names: MacDumont, Sean.
Title: Boats go! / Sean MacDumont.
Description: New York : Gareth Stevens Publishing, 2018. | Series: Ways to go | Includes index.
Identifiers: ISBN 9781538210130 (pbk.) | ISBN 9781538210154 (library bound) | ISBN 9781538210147 (6 pack)
Subjects: LCSH: Ships–Juvenile literature. | Boats and boating–Juvenile literature.
Classification: LCC VM150.M33 2018 | DDC 623.82–dc23

First Edition

Published in 2018 by
Gareth Stevens Publishing
111 East 14th Street, Suite 349
New York, NY 10003

Editor: Kate Mikoley
Designer: Sam DeMartin

Photo credits: Cover, p. 1 Thomas Barrat/Shutterstock.com; p. 5 IM_photo/Shutterstock.com; p. 7 project1photography/Shutterstock.com; p. 9 PAUL WASCHTSCHENKO/Shutterstock.com; pp. 11, 24 (dock) dasytnik/Shutterstock.com; p. 13 Alex Kolokythas Photography/Shutterstock.com; p. 15 Tanor/Shutterstock.com; p. 17 Leonard Zhukovsky/Shutterstock.com; p. 19 YanLev/Shutterstock.com; pp. 21, 24 (canoe) Phillip Rubino/Shutterstock.com; p. 23 glenda/Shutterstock.com; p. 24 (paddle) marekuliasz/Shutterstock.com.

Printed in the United States of America

CPSIA compliance information: Batch #CW18GS: For further information contact Gareth Stevens, New York, New York at 1-800-542-2595.

Contents

Boats go on water!

They go on oceans and rivers.

KANTAR

Boats take people many places.

They stop at docks.

Some boats move
things like food.

Big boats are called ships.

A cruise ship is
a big boat.

Some boats have sails.
Sails help the boat go.

Some boats are small.
A canoe is a small boat.

People row small boats.
Paddles help you row.

Words to Know

canoe

dock

paddle

Index